For Desirée

This project could not have happened without the
generous support of our friends, especially:
Robin Wildman — Editing
Laurie Caird — Layout
Dr. Raven Pfister — Editing
and our amazing Kickstarter backers

Desirée McCloud's name and likeness used with permission.
The story is a fictionalization of true events.
Any resemblance of other characters to actual persons living or
dead is entirely coincidental.

The demonstration depicted in this book involves fire.
Proper safety equipment and precautions should be used and
appropriate personnel involved before any attempt is made to
reproduce the demonstration.

First Printing

All sales inquiries should be directed to sales@mesii.com

ISBN# 978-1-950445-01-1

www.thewitchprincess.com

Cover Design by Mark Scherschel II and Laurie Caird

The Witch Princess

Author: Brittney Geleynse
Illustrator: Adrienne Silva
Adaptation: Sara Chandler
Layout and Font: Mark Scherschel II

In Memory of a True Story

There was once a
beautiful princess
named Desirée.

But Desirée didn't
want to be a princess.

She didn't want to wear frilly dresses and look the way she was told to look.

She didn't want to be well-mannered and act the way she was told to act.

She didn't want to do her royal duties and learn what she was told to learn.

She wanted to be...

She decorated herself with magic words and drawings to appear more like a witch.

She learned how to take care of rats.

She studied science and space to learn the magic of the stars, and read books about her favorite space witches and wizards.

But everyone still saw her as a beautiful princess.

Princess Desirée stopped behaving as a princess "ought to" and spoke her mind.

But her ideas were good and the people enjoyed hearing them.

In desperation, the Princess came up with one last plan.

She gathered a group of eighteen children together to teach them a fire spell.

If she could show them fire magic, then they would have no doubt that she was a witch!

Princess Desirée lit a candle and said,
"Is the candle burning?"

"Yes it is, Princess," the children responded.

Princess Desirée covered the candle
with a glass jar and watched
the last of the orange flame disappear.
"Is the fire out?" she asked.

"Yes it is, Princess," the children responded.

Princess Desirée yanked the jar away and the flame leapt back to life. The children all gasped!

"Do you think I'm a witch?"
Princess Desirée cackled hopefully.

"Yes, Witch Princess Desirée!" The children said, looking up at her with amazement.

Witch Princess Desirée was so happy
she danced a little dance.

"I must admit, it was no spell and no magic.
Fire needs three things to burn:

heat,

fuel,

and oxygen."

"I took away the fire's oxygen,
but just before it died, I added it back
and the fire flared back up."

"That is one of the many reasons fire is so amazing, but we have to be careful with it."

The children took hold of Witch Princess Desirée's hands and asked, "Can you teach us magic too?"

"Of course! I will teach you the science of the universe, and if you study hard enough, you will be able to do magic just like me."

And from that day forward, she was known as Witch Princess Desirée, perfectly a princess, wonderfully a witch, and happy to be herself.

The End

About Desirée K McCloud

Explorer, Student, Warrior, Princess, and Witch,
loved and missed.

Desirée, despite wearing a helmet, suffered brain injury in a cycling accident and died May 24, 2016 at the age of 27.

After her birth in Southern Indiana and graduation from Purdue University with a Behavioral Neuroscience degree, she made a home for herself in Seattle. She worked as a Research Associate providing services to pharmaceutical and biotech clients. Desirée was a strong advocate for women and for encouraging young girls to be whatever they wanted to be, founding Girl Scout Troop 42071 with Brittney Geleynse.

She loved *Star Wars*, sci-fi, and camping, and was loved for her intelligence, confidence, strong opinions, and desire to make the world a better place.

About Brittney Geleynse

Brittney created this story concept as a eulogy for her friend. It is based on true events from a Girl Scout meeting with the troop they co-founded. Brittney continues to run the troop with other friends of Desirée. When she isn't working with the girls, Brittney runs her toy store in Seattle. She lives with her husband Alan and their new daughter Ada.

About Adrienne Silva

Adrienne is a self-taught artist and illustrator who resides in Boise, Idaho. She is the resigned co-habitant with a gremlin named Mr. Kitty. She has many muscle and is very cool.

About Sara Chandler

Lab partners and friends, Sara and Desirée worked and played together in Seattle. Sara has since traded in her pipette for a keyboard and enjoys spending time reading comics with Pterodactyl the cat.

About Mark Scherschel II

Mark moved to Seattle with Desirée in 2011. He is proud and excited to have been able to work on this memorial project and create this font based on Desirée's handwriting.

Kickstarter Backers

The following are from the people who backed our Kickstarter campaign and helped make this book come to life. We are grateful for your support and patience as we worked our way to the completion of this book. Thank You!

Nathan, Alexz and Eric Chambers, Anonymous, Anonymous, Anonymous, Dan Borgerding, Randi, Laura J. Arnold, Rachael Velociraptor, Cody McCloud, Chris and Penny McCloud, Robin Wildman, C.C. Charles, Judy, Susan and Mark Scherschel, Sara, Jade, Lara, Jonathan, Liz, Tasha Turner, Brittney, Cameron, Elise and Nate, Josh, Ryan and Anna Rapp, Steve, Deckard Townes Herndon, Jack, Atta Dawahare, Sophia Bisignano-Vadino, Amy Lee, Jennifer Priester, Suzie Koons, Gloria Geleynse (GiGI), Aaron Perry, Alan, Fluff, Laurie Bramlage, James Thompson, Vijeta and Guillaume, Kayle, Purdue Fencing Club for a life time of connections, George Panayotov, The O'Getman's, Ragan A. Pitner, Jason Knichel, Anonymous, Michelle Vogel, Mary, Marissa, Allison, Anonymous, Betty, Dillon, Matilda Senik-Puckett, Anne, Mahesh, Warren, William, Bunnies, Fred Comeau Jr., Anonymous, Autumn Friel, Mariano G Lizano Alpizar, Alex Ashley James and Pip the Keeshond Pup, Leilani Bales, Deanne Kludy, Jesse N Hirschmann, Newton and Turing, Isabella, Anne and Beatrice, Tara Kent, Kimberly Johnson, Donna McCloud, Amy Cadwallader, Gigi, Sage Curtis, Mary/Emmari Corrales, Emily Ivie, Lincoln Swanson, Trevor A. Ramirez, Travis, Joslyn Dresser, Jamie Swedler, Love from Grandma Sharon, John and Dianne Pitner, Walka Family, Sara G., Whitney Jacky, Scott Geleynse, Stephanie Nelson, Tatiana Amor, Jolie Vrabel, Waspark, Matthew Varley, Mathew and Pat Scherschel, Josh Sara and Jim of Everett, Yvan Martino, Anonymous, Anonymous, Anonymous, Sayed, Tiago, Anonymous, Jace, Julie, John, Emily Rice, Adam Tierney, Anonymous, Kyle E. Andersen

CPSIA information can be obtained
at www.ICGtesting.com
Printed in the USA
BVHW021207240919
559214BV00002B/6/P

For Desirée

This project could not have happened without the
generous support of our friends, especially:
Robin Wildman — Editing
Laurie Caird — Layout
Dr. Raven Pfister — Editing
and our amazing Kickstarter backers

Desirée McCloud's name and likeness used with permission.
The story is a fictionalization of true events.
Any resemblance of other characters to actual persons living
or dead is entirely coincidental.
The demonstration depicted in this book involves fire.
Proper safety equipment and precautions should be used and
appropriate personnel involved before any attempt is made to
reproduce the demonstration.

First Printing

All sales inquiries should be directed to sales@mesii.com

ISBN# 978-1-950445-00-4

www.thewitchprincess.com

The Witch Princess

Author: Brittney Geleynse
Illustrator: Adrienne Silva
Adaptation: Sara Chandler
Layout and Font: Mark Scherschel II

In Memory of a True Story

There was once a
beautiful princess
named Desirée.

But Desirée didn't
want to be a princess.

She didn't want to wear frilly dresses
and look the way she was told to look.

She didn't
want to be
well-mannered
and act the
way she was
told to act.

She didn't
want to do her
royal duties
and learn what
she was told
to learn.

She wanted to be...

...a witch!

So Princess Desirée did everything she could to turn into a witch.

She decorated herself with magic words
and drawings to appear more like a witch.

She learned how to take care of rats.

She studied science and space to learn the magic of the stars, and read books about her favorite space witches and wizards.

But everyone still saw her as a beautiful princess.

Princess Desirée stopped behaving as a princess "ought to" and spoke her mind.

But her ideas were good and the people enjoyed hearing them.

Princess Desirée tried being "bossy", hoping people thought witches were bossy.

But the people thought she was a good leader and respected her ability to make decisions.

In desperation, the Princess
came up with one last plan.

She gathered a group of eighteen children together to teach them a fire spell.

If she could show them fire magic, then they would have no doubt that she was a witch!

Princess Desirée lit a candle and said,
"Is the candle burning?"

"Yes it is, Princess," the children responded.

Princess Desirée covered the candle
with a glass jar and watched
the last of the orange flame disappear.
"Is the fire out?" she asked.

"Yes it is, Princess," the children responded.

Princess Desirée yanked the jar away and the flame leapt back to life. The children all gasped!

"Do you think I'm a witch?"
Princess Desirée cackled hopefully.

"Yes, Witch Princess Desirée!" The children said, looking up at her with amazement.

Witch Princess Desirée was so happy
she danced a little dance.

"Would you like to know how I made that magic, children? I will tell you as long as you promise to always call me Witch Princess Desirée."

"Yes, Witch Princess Desirée! Please tell us
how you performed that spell."

"I must admit, it was no spell and no magic.
Fire needs three things to burn:

fuel,

heat,

and oxygen."

"I took away the fire's oxygen, but just before it died, I added it back and the fire flared back up."

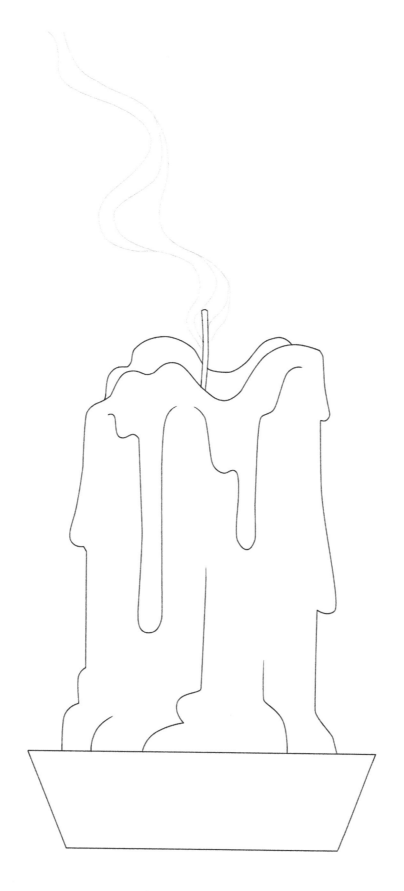

"That is one of the many reasons fire is so amazing, but we have to be careful with it."

The children took hold of Witch Princess Desirée's hands and asked, "Can you teach us magic too?"

"Of course! I will teach you the science of the universe, and if you study hard enough, you will be able to do magic just like me."

And from that day forward, she was known as Witch Princess Desirée, perfectly a princess, wonderfully a witch, and happy to be herself.

About Desirée K McCloud

Explorer, Student, Warrior, Princess, and Witch,
loved and missed.

Desirée, despite wearing a helmet, suffered brain injury in a cycling accident and died May 24, 2016 at the age of 27.

After her birth in Southern Indiana and graduation from Purdue University with a Behavioral Neuroscience degree, she made a home for herself in Seattle. She worked as a Research Associate providing services to pharmaceutical and biotech clients. Desirée was a strong advocate for women and for encouraging young girls to be whatever they wanted to be, founding Girl Scout Troop 42071 with Brittney Geleynse.

She loved *Star Wars*, sci-fi, and camping, and was loved for her intelligence, confidence, strong opinions, and desire to make the world a better place.

About Brittney Geleynse
Brittney created this story concept as a eulogy for her friend. It is based on true events from a Girl Scout meeting with the troop they co-founded. Brittney continues to run the troop with other friends of Desirée. When she isn't working with the girls, Brittney runs her toy store in Seattle. She is happily married to Alan and they are expecting their first child.

About Adrienne Silva
Adrienne is a self-taught artist and illustrator who resides in Boise, Idaho. She is the resigned co-habitant with a gremlin named Mr. Kitty. She has many muscle and is very cool.

About Sara Chandler
Lab partners and friends, Sara and Desirée worked and played together in Seattle. Sara has since traded in her pipette for a keyboard and enjoys spending time reading comics with Pterodactyl the cat.

About Mark Scherschel II
Mark moved to Seattle with Desirée in 2011. He is proud and excited to have been able to work on this memorial project and create this font based on Desirée's handwriting.